MOLE MOVES HOUSE

For all our godchildren
E.B.   G.B.

First published in Great Britain in 1998 by
Macdonald Young Books
an imprint of Wayland Publishers Ltd
61 Western Road
Hove
East Sussex
BN3 1JD

Text copyright © Elizabeth Buchanan 1989
Illustrations copyright © George Buchanan 1998

Find Macdonald Young Books on the internet at
http://www.myb.co.uk

Printed and bound in Portugal
by Edições ASA

British Library Cataloguing in Publication Data
available.

ISBN: 0 7500 2552 2

MOLE MOVES HOUSE

Elizabeth & George Buchanan

MACDONALD YOUNG BOOKS

When Mole first noticed Mr Carrington at work in the garden, he knew at once that he had found a man after his own heart. Mr Carrington was digging and he was doing a very good job.

Mole thought how proud he would be to work with such a good digger. He saw how much work there was to be done and imagined how delighted Mr Carrington would be to have skilled help.

So Mole decided to move house right away.
He would become Mr Carrington's neighbour.

On his first day
as Mr Carrington's
new neighbour,
Mole helped to enlarge
the vegetable patch.

He could tell that
Mr Carrington was
surprised.

The next day Mole dug a new vegetable patch.
Mr Carrington was amazed. That night Mr
Carrington decided to do something for Mole.

Mr Carrington worked all night long...

...to finish the trap he was making.

When Mole woke up in the morning, it was his turn to be surprised. A fine new gate had been fitted over his biggest molehill!

Mole tucked his bootscraper into a convenient position by the gate and set off in a hurry. One good turn deserves another, and the herb garden was definitely too small. Mole planned to do some fast digging there!

As time went on Mr Carrington found
more and more to do for Mole.

He spent days designing a system
to flood Mole's largest galleries with water.

Then he set up a pump and a hose leading to Mole's house.

Mole found some pipes and nozzles and set to work with a mole wrench to do some plumbing. What a luxury to have running water in his home!

In return for this kindness, Mole did a really good job
excavating the flower bed.

Mr Carrington went to a lot of trouble to discover which wood burnt with the most choking black smoke. He lit a fire in the barbecue and puffed smoke in at the back of the molehill.

Mole got busy at
once. Hooks were
required, and
pulleys and pipes —
and some vents.

Very quickly he was able to install a smokery behind his kitchen. Smoked worms were Mole's favourite supper!

That summer Mole dug the strawberry plot very thoroughly. Mr Carrington spoke to a local farmer who had heard that moles dislike loud music.

Mr Carrington buried
stereos and loudspeakers
and other sound equipment
near Mole's home.

There was music everywhere!
Mole was very happy.

Sometimes he played along on his cornet during the long summer evenings.

Mole used every corner of
the garden to demonstrate
his talents as a digger.

Eventually Mr Carrington
came to rely on him
completely. He would
relax with his family,

trusting that Mole would do a quality job in the garden.

By autumn, Mr Carrington could not think of
anything else to do for Mole. There was not
much to be done in the garden, and there didn't
seem to be enough room in the house anymore.
So, the Carringtons decided to move.

The whole family began to look for a new house.
When Mr Carrington said, "This is the place!"
Mole was just as excited as the rest of the family.

It was a good, big house,
surrounded by lawns. Mr
Carrington could imagine
a vegetable patch at the
back. So could Mole.

It takes a lot of hard work to move house.
Everything must be carefully packed before
the furniture and boxes are loaded into the
removal van. There was work for everyone.

Mole didn't have
a moment to spare
as he scurried from
molehill to van with
piles of his belongings.

Imagine his horror as he brought up the last load
to discover that his family had forgotten him!

Bounding on to his bicycle,
Mole tore off after the van.
Before long he caught sight
of it ahead, waiting in a
traffic jam. With a whoop
of joy, Mole overtook the
tractors, cars and lorries
waiting at the busy junction.

He overtook the
removal van and
streaked ahead,
down the road
to his new home.

Mole took one look at the smooth green lawn. It was clear Mr Carrington was going to need a great deal of help. There was no time to lose.

When the Carringtons arrived a few minutes later, they were just in time to see Mole finishing his first molehill in the new garden.

Mole was pleased.

He could tell that Mr Carrington was surprised.